Spots and Stripes

written by Pam Holden
illustrated by Pauline Whimp

1

"Look! I have spots," said the giraffe.

"Look!
I have stripes,"
said the tiger.

"We have stripes, too," said the bees.

"Look! We have
spots, too,"
said the butterflies.

9

"Look! We have
stripes, too,"
said the zebras.

"We have spots, too,"
said the ladybugs.

"Look! We have
spots **and** stripes,"
said the snakes.

"We have spots **and** stripes, too! SSSSSSSSsssssssss!"